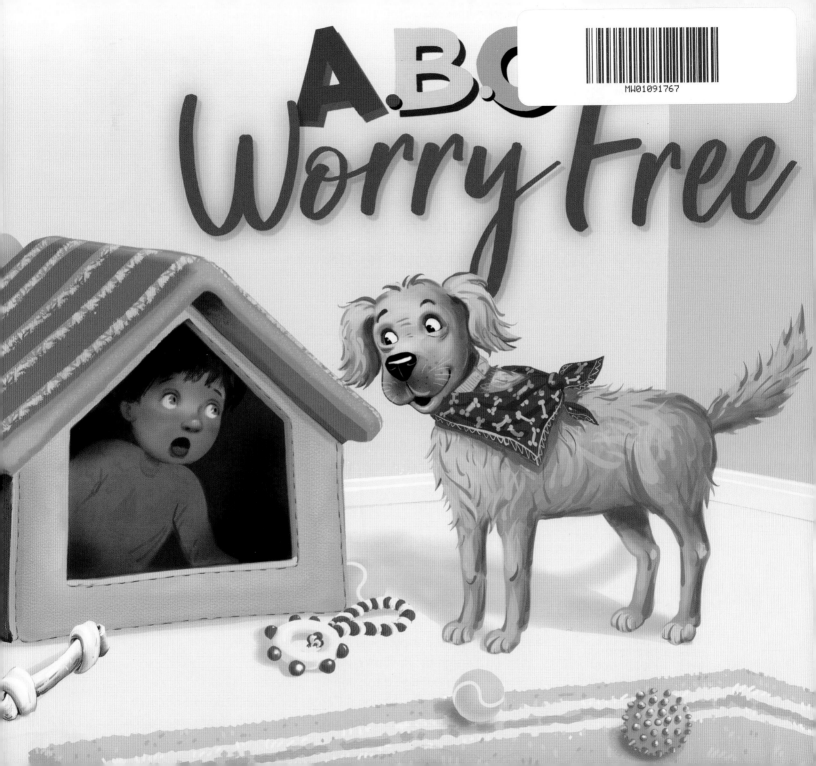

A.B.C
Worry Free

To my family and students…
you are stronger than your fears.

DUPLICATION AND COPYRIGHT

NATIONAL CENTER for
YOUTH ISSUES

P.O. Box 22185
Chattanooga, TN 37422-2185
423.899.5714 • 866.318.6294
fax: 423.899.4547 • www.ncyi.org

ISBN: 978-1-937870-54-6 $9.95
Library of Congress Control Number: 2018960232
© 2018 National Center for Youth Issues, Chattanooga, TN
All rights reserved.
Written by: Noel Foy
Illustrations by: Olga and Aleksey Ivanov
Design by: Phillip W. Rodgers
Contributing Editor: Jennifer Deshler
Published by National Center for Youth Issues • Softcover
Printed at Starkey Printing, Chattanooga, Tennessee, U.S.A., October 2018

There was nothing Max enjoyed more than playing outside with his friends. Today, they played his favorite game of all, Hide 'n Seek.

"One…two…three…," Casey shouted as Max and Sam sprinted to hide.

Sam hid behind a large rock.

Max crouched between two large bushes.

"Ready or not! Here I come!" Casey shouted
as she ran to find her friends.

Max peered through the bushes and thought, *Best. Hiding spot. Ev-er!*

But little did Max know, something else lurked in the bushes that day.

Uh-oh! Guess who found Max first? A swarm of bees!

"Ouch! Stop! Help!" cried Max.

But the bees would not listen and flew right up his shirt!

Max ran inside screaming, *"I GOT STUNG!"*

His mom rushed to his side with an ice pack, as their dog Snuffy fetched Max a box of tissues.

"I'm never playing outside again!" Max sobbed, wiping his tears.

"I know it hurts," said Max's mom, comforting him with a warm hug, "but playing inside forever doesn't sound very fun."

"We'll see about that!" Max bawled.

That night, Max couldn't sleep. At last, he turned to Snuffy, who lay in her doghouse beside Max's bed. *"What am I gonna do Snuffy? How will I tell my friends I'm afraid to play outside?"*

Snuffy was busy chewing on a dog bone, and it gave Max an idea. *"That's it Snuffy! I'll just say I'm busy!"*

The following day, when Casey asked Max to ride bikes, can you guess what Max said? *"Oh, I'm busy today. I have to clean my room."*

But do you think Max really cleaned his room? Nope! He just sat by the window and watched his friends ride bikes.

The next day wasn't so different. When Sam asked him to play street hockey, can you guess what Max told him? *"Sorry… I'm busy. I have to check my dog for fleas."*

But do you think Max *really* checked Snuffy for fleas? Nope! Once again, he sat by the window and watched his friends play outside.

"It must be tough watching your friends have fun without you," said Max's mom. "I bet they'd understand how you feel. Why don't you go out and join them?"

But all Max could think was, *Why don't I jump in a beehive while I'm at it?!*

Later that afternoon, Max found his older brother, Chris, teaching Snuffy a new trick.

"Snuffy, fetch!" Chris commanded.

In a flash, Snuffy darted to the kitchen and returned with a box of cookies. "Way to go, Snuffy!" exclaimed Chris, handing her a treat.

"How'd she learn that?" asked Max.

"Ah, it's just a little trick I taught her. You'd be surprised what you can teach someone with the right attitude."

"Do you think you could teach someone to worry less?"

Chris chuckled. "Absolutely. As long as they're not afraid to learn something new."

Easy for him to say, Max thought. *He's not afraid of anything.*

13

On the bus ride home from school the next day, Max sat by himself at the front of the bus. His friends were at the back, in their usual spot.

"What's up with Max?" asked Casey. "First he won't play with us. Now he won't sit with us?"

"I know!" Sam huffed. "Do you think he needs our help?"

They both looked at Max sitting all alone. What could they do? Suddenly, a thought crept into Casey's head… "I have an idea!"

When Max got home, he heard a loud KNOCK, KNOCK.

He opened the door to find Sam and Casey.
Can you guess what they asked him to play? HIDE 'N SEEK!

Max was so excited he jumped right out of his sneakers!

But Max quickly remembered what happened the last time he'd played outside.
"Sorry, I can't today. I have to help my sister organize her sock drawer."

But do you think Max *really* helped his sister organize her sock drawer?
Let's not be ridiculous! For the third straight day, he sat by the window and
watched his friends play outside.

But today was even worse—they were playing his favorite game of all!

"This stinks!" Max shouted.

He wandered into his brother's bedroom where Chris was teaching Snuffy a new high five trick.

"Can I play with you guys?" he asked.

"Sure," said Chris. "But wouldn't you rather be playing Hide 'n Seek with your friends?"

"I'm never playing outside again," Max mumbled.

"But you love Hide 'n Seek!"

Max shook his head. *"Not since I got stung by that bee!"*

"Hmmm. I think it's time you learned a little trick that helped me overcome my fear."

Max's jaw dropped to the floor. *"You?? You're not afraid of anything!"*

Chris chuckled. "Of course I am. I used to be afraid of dogs, if you can believe it."

"Dogs!" cried Max. *"But you're not afraid of Snuffy!"*

Chris smiled. "Not anymore. Thanks to A.B.C. Worry Free."

"A.B.C. Worry Free?" asked Max. *"How does it work?"*

"It all starts with the letter **A**," Chris began. "**A** stands for **Accept**. You have to accept your fears in order to face them. It's perfectly normal to be afraid of bees, but if we let fear stop us from doing what we love, we're worrying too much."

"**B** stands for **Breathe**," Chris continued. "Remember to take slow, deep breaths when you're feeling anxious. I like to imagine I'm smelling something amazing, like this pizza."

Chris held a slice to his nose and inhaled a deep *Snnnnnn* for the count of one…two…three…

"Now, let's cool it down," and he exhaled a slow *Haaaaah* as he counted back from three …two…one…

21

"Now you try," he said.

Max inhaled a deep *Snnnnnn* and blew out a slow *Haaaaah* to cool off his own slice of yummy pizza.

"Now, you're ready for the third letter," said Chris. "**C** stands for **Change**.

To face our fears, it helps to change the way we think about them. Instead of worrying about getting stung, imagine all the fun you'll have playing outside with your friends. Does that make sense?"

"*I think so . . .*" said Max. "*You're saying I need to **Accept** my fear, **Breathe** to stay calm, and **Change** my thoughts when I'm worried.*"

"That's it!" Chris exclaimed, high-fiving Max and Snuffy. "But make sure to practice this when you're not scared. That way, you'll be ready when you are."

The next morning, Max got busy practicing his new trick. "**A for *Accept*, B for Breathe, C for Change**," he kept repeating. "**A for *Accept*, B for…**"

Just then, something buzzed above Max's head. *"It can't be,"* he thought. *"I'm **inside!**"* But sure enough, it was! A bee in Max's bedroom!!

Max was so scared he hid inside Snuffy's doghouse. He even started panting like a dog! His heart beat like a drum as all of his old fears came rushing back. But *this time*, Max knew how to face them.

Boldly, Max crawled out from the doghouse, finally willing to **Accept** his fear.

"It's okay to feel scared," he said to himself as he got dressed.

Next, he took several deep **_Breaths_** to stay calm..

Lastly, he **Changed** his way of thinking. *"I can handle my worry,"* he told the bee. *"I'll stay out of your nest, and you stay out of mine!"*

The bee didn't like being spoken to that way, so it circled Max's head and buzzed noisily around his ear. But Max stood tall and exclaimed, "No more missing fun with my friends!"

The bee was so scared he flew right out the window.

Max burst through the door and ran outside to join his friends once more.

"Ready or not, here I come!" he shouted.

Tips for Parents and Educators...

No one wants to see children experience anxiety. We may even want to eliminate it from their lives. However, avoiding tests, games, recitals, social situations or stressful triggers can deprive children of opportunities to practice valuable skills and can actually reinforce fears in the long run. Some anxiety is common, but when it is persistent and interferes with daily life, children are worrying too much. This book is a response to the rise in anxiety in children from all backgrounds and its impact on learning, relationships, executive function, and wellness.

Children need to know anxiety is nothing to be ashamed of and is a normal reaction to real or imagined dangers. Common stressors include fear of mistakes, imperfection, performance and pressures related to school, relationships, social media and overly busy schedules. In today's world, many children's stress responses are *over-active*, sending them into fight, flight, or freeze mode multiple times a day, which can look like the following:

• **Fight**: punching, pushing, spitting, glaring, breaking an item, mean words

• **Flight**: spacing out, avoidance, excessive fidgeting, trips to the bathroom

• **Freeze**: inflexibility, frozen stares, difficulty seeing a new perspective

We must teach children to calm their minds and bodies and recognize their thoughts, words, actions, feelings and physical symptoms when anxious.

Do's and Don'ts for Communicating with Anxious Children

Do use a calm tone and validate feelings	Don't belittle or amplify feelings
• I know you're scared. I'm here to support you through this. • I can understand why that would be worrisome. I've felt that way before. • I'm glad you're sharing-tell me more.	• Don't worry about it. • You shouldn't feel that way. • Just put on your big girl/boy pants. • It's no big deal. • Get over it.

Other tips to help children decrease and take charge of their anxiety:

• Express confidence in your child's ability to learn coping skills.

• Involve your child in the solution making process once he/she is calm.

• Your child will fail at times. View mistakes as opportunities to learn.

• Life will throw curve balls-use If/Then frames to make a Plan B (i.e. If mom doesn't pick me up from practice, then I will talk to the coach).

• Model healthy use of screen time, social media and coping skills (i.e. breathing exercises, visualization, mindfulness and Cognitive Behavioral Therapy)

For more information about teaching and parenting anxious children, visit www.ammpe.com